The Passover Parrot

MATZA

Evelyn Zusman
Illustrations by **Kyrsten Brooker**

KAR-BEN
PUBLISHING

KAR-BEN PUBLISHING, INC.
A division of Lerner Publishing Group, Inc.
241 First Avenue North
Minneapolis, MN 55401 USA
1-800-4-KARBEN
Website address: www.karben.com

Library of Congress Cataloging-in-Publication Data

Names: Zusman, Evelyn, author. | Brooker, Kyrsten, illustrator.
Title: The Passover parrot / by Evelyn Zusman ; illustrated by Kyrsten Brooker.
Description: Revised edition. | Minneapolis : Kar-Ben Publishing, [2017] | Ages 3–8, K
    to grade 3. | Summary: Relates what happens when the family parrot steals the
    afikomen at the Passover seder.
Identifiers: LCCN 2017029236 (print) | LCCN 2016059661 (ebook) | ISBN
    9781512428841 (eb pdf) | ISBN 9781512428827 (lb : alk. paper) | ISBN
    9781512428834 (pb : alk. paper)
Subjects: | CYAC: Passover—Fiction. | Judaism—Customs and practices—Fiction. |
    Parrots—Fiction. | Jews—United States—Fiction.
Classification: LCC PZ7.Z84 (print) | LCC PZ7.Z84 Pas 2017 (ebook) | DDC [E]—dc23
LC record available at https://lccn.loc.gov/2017029236

Manufactured in the United States of America
1-41565-23390-6/22/2017

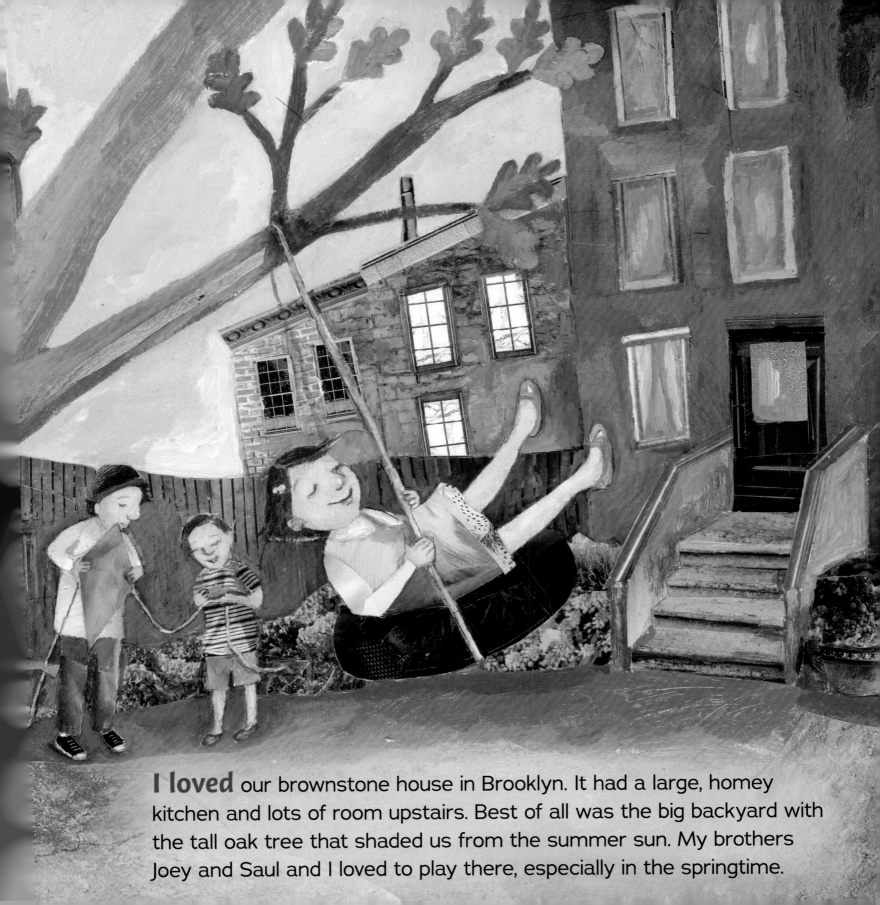

I loved our brownstone house in Brooklyn. It had a large, homey kitchen and lots of room upstairs. Best of all was the big backyard with the tall oak tree that shaded us from the summer sun. My brothers Joey and Saul and I loved to play there, especially in the springtime.

One day our neighbor, Mrs. Brown, knocked on our door.

"Good morning," Mama said. "What's that you're holding? Your parrot!"

"Yes, Mrs. Cohen. I'm moving. Wouldn't you like to keep him?" She noticed me, tugging at Mama's skirt, and pushed the cage into my hand. "For you, Lily, a present."

And before Mama could say, "Seven children and a parrot!"
Mrs. Brown was gone.

I jumped with such delight that I scared the parrot
half to death. Mama shook her head. "More
things to take care of," she grumbled.

"I'll help you, Mama. You'll see."

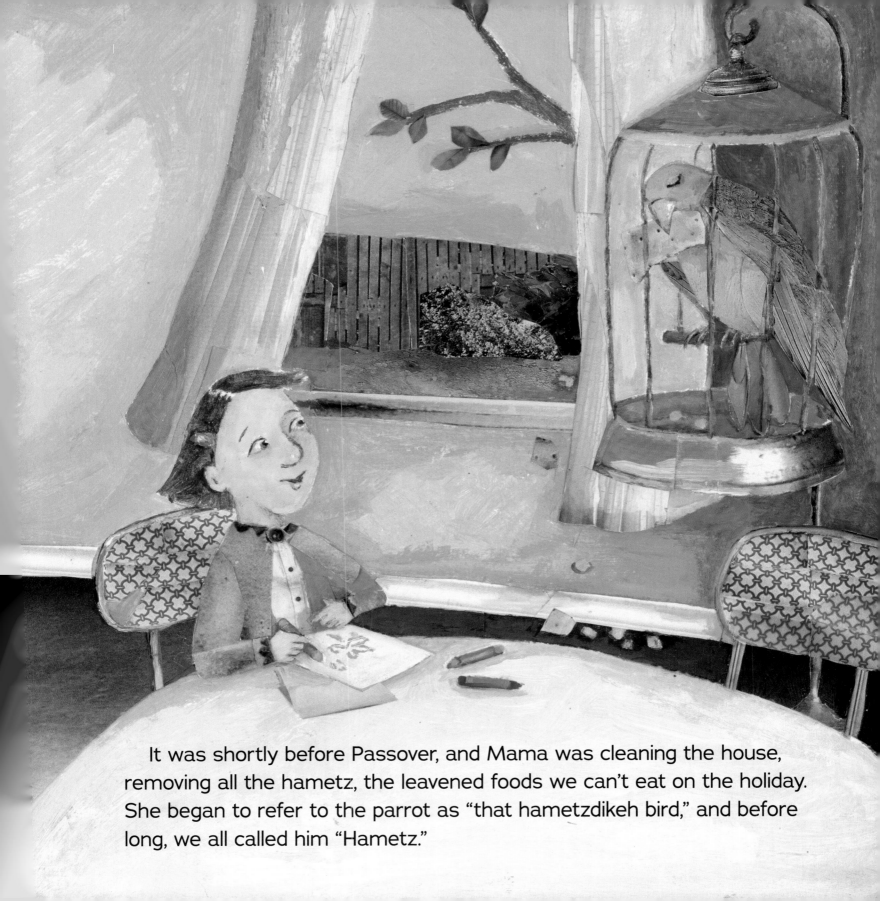

It was shortly before Passover, and Mama was cleaning the house, removing all the hametz, the leavened foods we can't eat on the holiday. She began to refer to the parrot as "that hametzdikeh bird," and before long, we all called him "Hametz."

"Can you say the Four Questions in Hebrew?" Papa asked me a few days before the seder.

His smile seemed to say, "It's okay if you can't." But Joey was old enough to ask them in English, so I made up my mind to learn them in Hebrew.

"Mama, will you listen to me say the Four Questions?" I asked. But Mama was too busy. "Ask Joey to listen to you."

I asked Joey.

"Why me?" he said. "Ask Saul or Rachel or Franny."

"Never mind," I replied.

In the end I chose Hametz. He was never too busy to listen. In fact he loved it when I practiced.

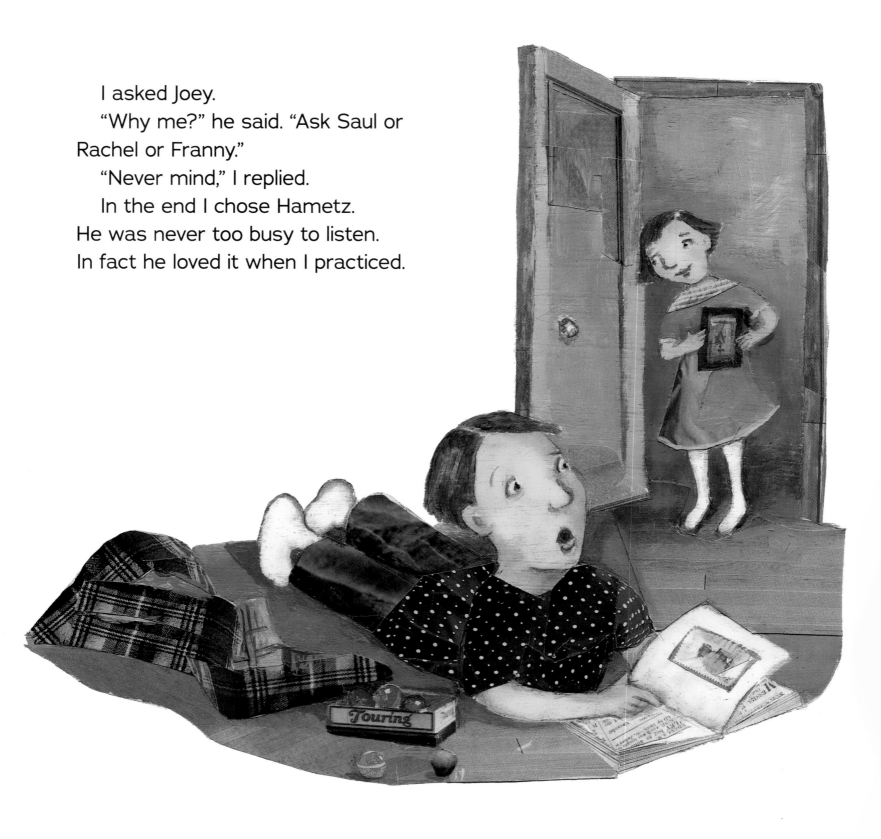

"Mah nishtanah halailah hazeh . . ."

I sang. And Hametz repeated in
his parrot-squeaky voice:

"Mah nishtanah halailah hazeh . . ."

"Mi kol halaylot," I continued.

"Mi kol halaylot," squeaked the parrot.

Would Papa be surprised!
I could hardly wait for the seder.

At last the day came. David and Franny helped Mama in the kitchen. Rachel and Saul set the table. Joey, Becky, and I checked that everything was in order.

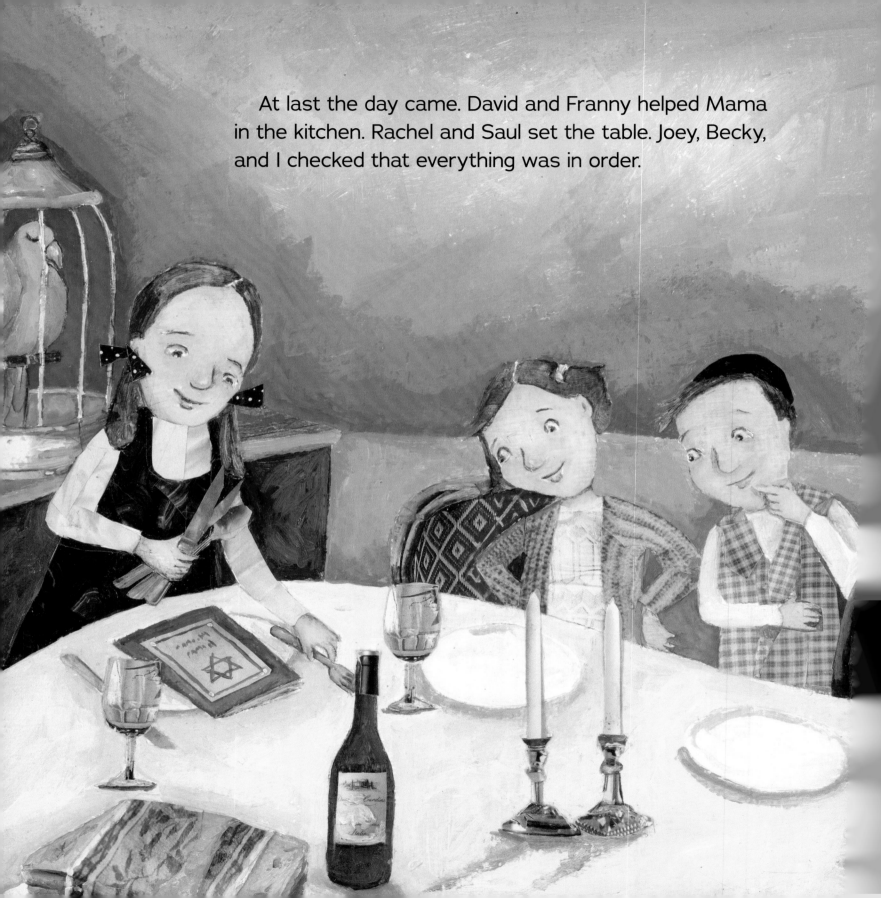

"Haggadot?" Joey asked.

"Check," I said.

"Charoset?"

"Mmm!" Becky said, sampling some.

"Wine?"

"Enough for every cup and Elijah's, too," Papa called from the kitchen.

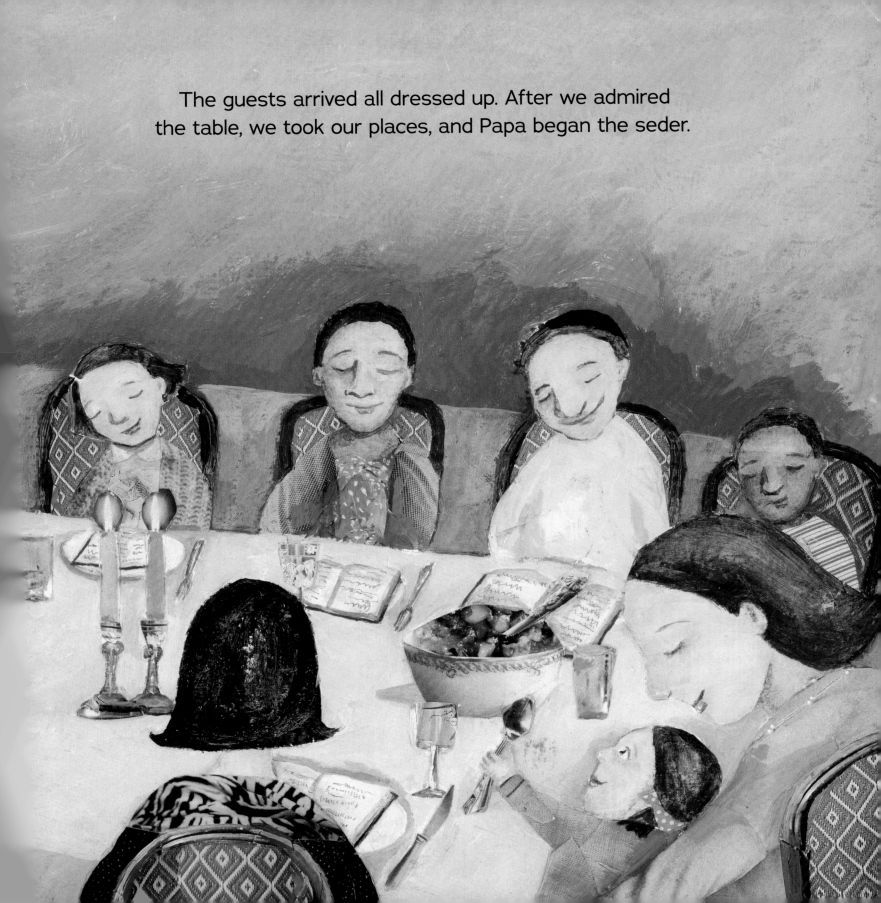

The guests arrived all dressed up. After we admired
the table, we took our places, and Papa began the seder.

He broke the middle matzah and put half back under the satin cover. He wrapped the other half in a napkin.

"This is the afikomen," he said, putting it behind the pillow on his chair. "Whoever brings it to me after dinner will get a reward."

We all smiled.
Joey laughed. He had already taken the afikomen.
"Here, Lily. Hide it quickly," he whispered.

I snatched the napkin with the afikomen and ran upstairs to my bedroom. As I slipped back into my seat, Papa called, "Quiet, everyone. Lily will ask the Four Questions."

I stood on a chair and began to sing:
"Mah nishtanah halailah hazeh . . ."
And as I paused to take a breath, Hametz, who had been sitting quietly in his cage in the living room, repeated in his squeaky parrot voice:

"Mah nishtanah halailah hazeh . . ."

All eyes turned to Hametz. I tried to continue.

"**Mi kol halaylot.**"

The parrot squeaked right after me, "**Mi kol halaylot.**" My brothers giggled. The guests laughed, too.

"Take the parrot up to the bedroom," Papa ordered.

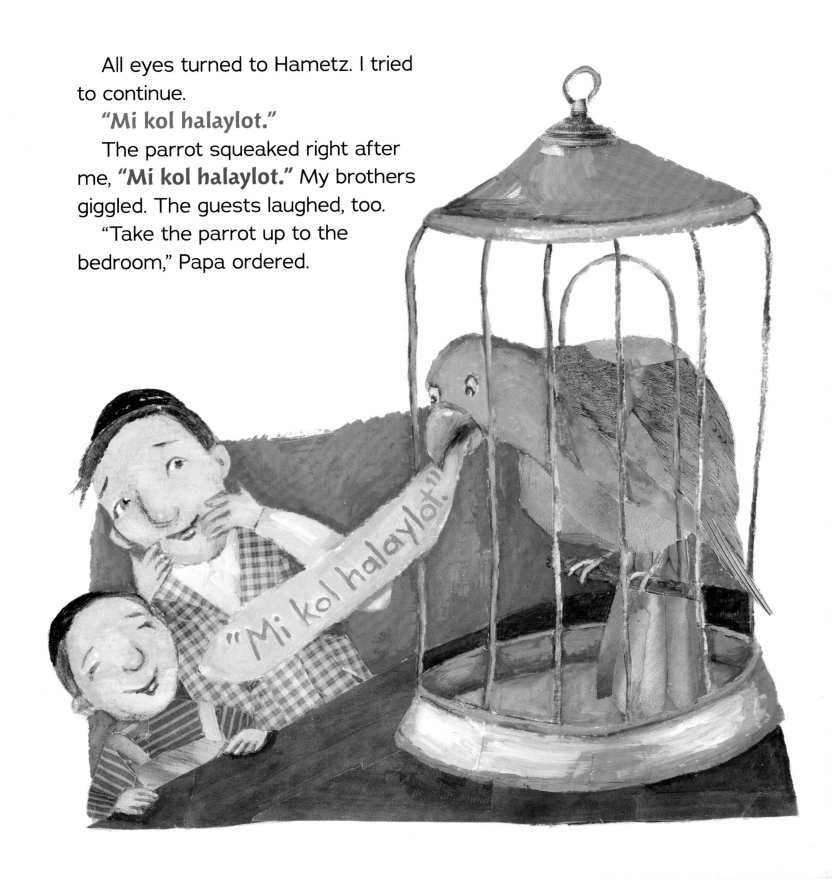

When I came back I sang the Four Questions without a single mistake. The guests clapped, and Papa smiled.

With the sweet singing and the delicious meal, I forgot about the parrot.

At last, Papa called for the afikomen so we could finish the Seder.

"Joey, do you have it?"
"No, Papa."
"Saul, do you have it?"
"No, Papa."
"Lily?"
"Yes, Papa."
"May I have the afikomen please?"

I ran to my bedroom, but there was no afikomen.
I looked under the table and under the bed.
No afikomen. And there was no parrot, either.
The cage door was wide open and Hametz was gone.

I sat down on the floor and began to cry. Papa sent Joey, and he searched, too. Then came Saul. In a minute, he knew exactly what had happened.

"Follow me," he said.

Joey and I followed him down the stairs, through the kitchen, and out the back door into the yard.

There was Hametz, perched on a branch of our tall oak tree, holding the afikomen tightly in his beak.

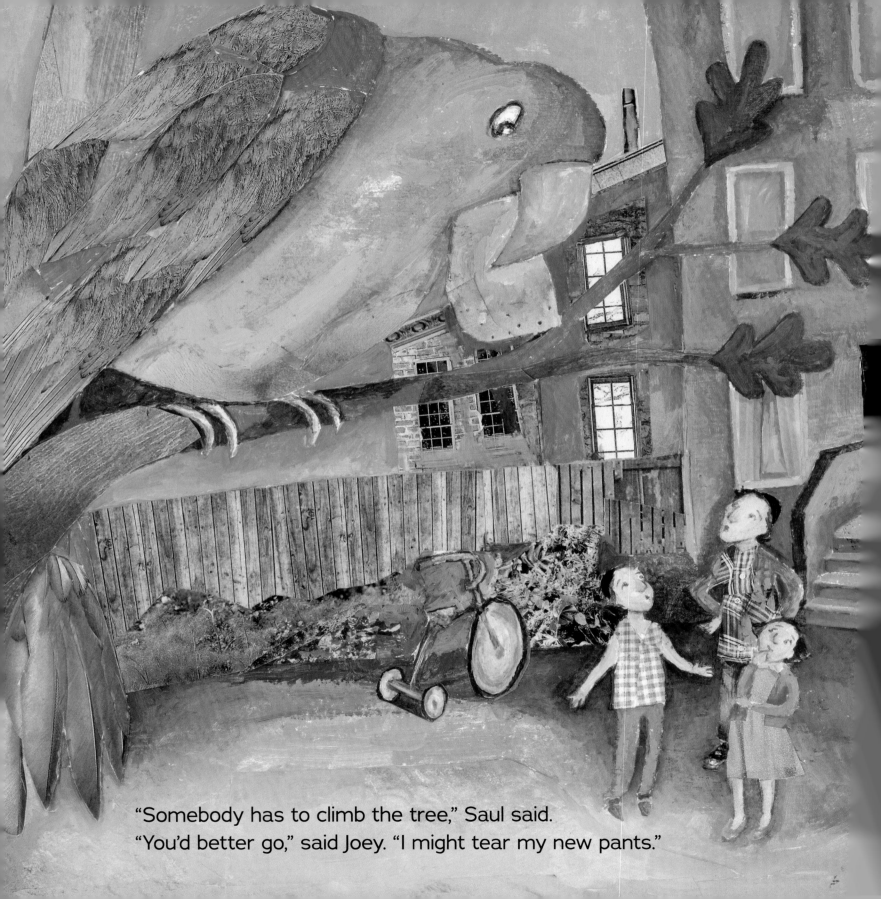

"Somebody has to climb the tree," Saul said.
"You'd better go," said Joey. "I might tear my new pants."

"No, don't go," I said. "Just let me talk to Hametz."
Then, at the top of my lungs, I sang as loudly as I could,

Hametz couldn't resist. He opened his beak and repeated, **"Mah nishtanah . . ."** The afikomen dropped.

Did Joey catch it? Did Saul?
No! I caught it myself! Well, what was left of it. When
I turned around, the whole family and all our guests
were standing behind me, watching and clapping.

As we returned to the house to finish the seder, we heard echoes of a squeaky voice singing, **"Mah nishtanah . . ."** Hametz had flown quietly back through the window into the cage. Perched on one leg, he was practicing for the second night's seder.